God Gave Us Love

by Lisa Tawn Bergren · art by Laura J. Bryant

WATERBROOK
PRESS

To Liv, Emma, and Jack, with all the love possible in a mama's heart

GOD GAVE US LOVE

All Scripture quotations or paraphrases are taken from the Holy Bible, New International Version®. NIV®. Copyright © 1973, 1978, 1984 by International Bible Society. Used by permission of Zondervan Publishing House. All rights reserved.

Hardcover ISBN 978-1-4000-7447-1
eBook ISBN 978-0-307-73084-8

Text copyright © 2009 by Lisa Tawn Bergren
Illustrations copyright © 2009 by Laura Bryant, www.laurabryant.com

Published in the United States by WaterBrook, an imprint of the Crown Publishing Group, a division of Penguin Random House LLC, New York.

WATERBROOK® and its deer colophon are registered trademarks of Penguin Random House LLC.

Library of Congress Cataloging-in-Publication Data.
Bergren, Lisa Tawn.
    God gave us love / by Lisa Tawn Bergren ; art by Laura J. Bryant. —1st ed.
        p. cm.
    Summary: Grampa Bear tells Little Cub all about God's love and why she should be patient, gentle, kind, and loving to family members and others, even when she does not like them very much.
    ISBN 978-1-4000-7447-1
    [1. Love—Fiction. 2. God—Love—Fiction. 3. Christian life—Fiction. 4. Polar bear—Fiction.
5. Bears—Fiction.] I. Bryant, Laura J., ill.
II. Title.
    PZ7.B452233Gol 2009
    [E]—dc22
                                    2009004093

Printed in the United States of America
2017

10 9 8

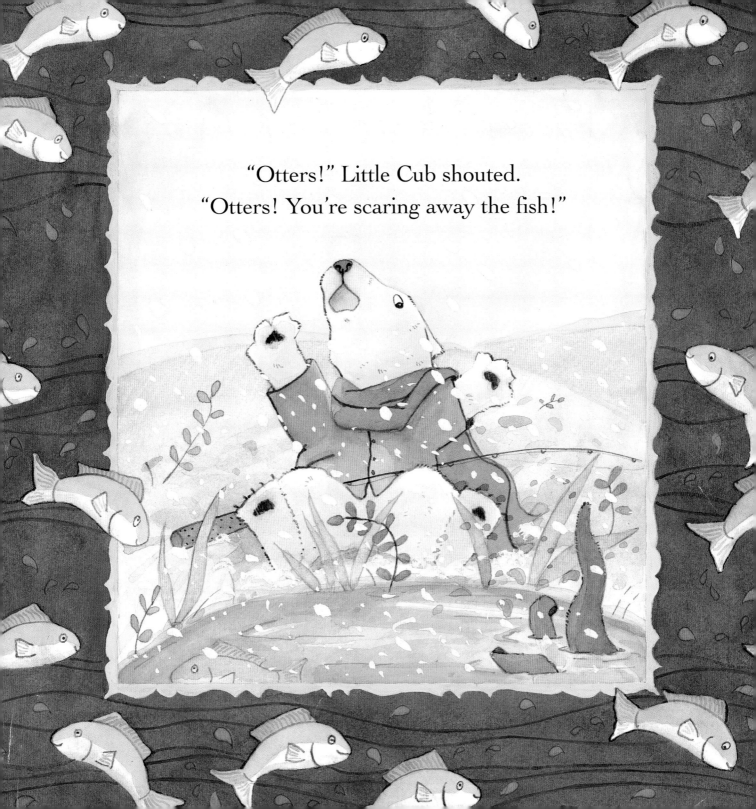

"Otters!" Little Cub shouted.
"Otters! You're scaring away the fish!"

"Easy, Little Cub," Grampa said. "The otters can share our spot."

"But Grampa," Little Cub complained, "if they scare all the fish away, we won't get any."

"That's all right," he said. "Half the fun of fishing is being together, right?"

"I...guess so."

"You know, Little Cub," Grampa said, "God wants us to show the otters love… He wants us to show everyone his love."

Little Cub thought on that awhile. "I love the otters. I just don't like them right now."

Grampa laughed. "I know *that* feeling."

"I always like *and* love you, Grampa,"
Little Cub said. "But why?"

"It's something deep within us,
something I can't totally explain—
only that God is love, so he created
us to love.

He ties us all together like the
strings on our snowshoes, heart
to heart."

"I don't wanna love the otters like Mama and Papa love each other," Little Cub said. "You know, all that kissy and huggy stuff."

Grampa smiled. "The love between mamas and papas is a special kind of love, given by God. Someday you may even like it."

"God gave us love, all kinds of love.
The love of mamas and papas,
the love between friends and family.
And his love too."

"His love brings out the best in us, and families show us love all the time," Grampa said.

"Group hug!" Little Cub yelled, and her sister and brother came running to join in.

They stood there for a bit.
It felt warm and cozy and *close*.

"I think *this* is God bringing out
the best in us," said Little Cub.
"I think this is God giving us love."

"Any time we show love,
Little Cub, we're sharing
a bit of his love."

"How come one minute I love these two and the next minute I feel like they're a couple of pesky otters?" Little Cub asked.

"Because while we *want* to love others as God loves us, we don't always *feel* like loving them. But when we choose to, it's always the right thing."

"God gave us love so we could see goodness in others, even when they make us grumpy."

"I know, I know," Little Cub said with a sigh. "God gave us love."

"Little Cub! God reminds us to show others love
by being patient, gentle, and kind," said Grampa.
"In all ways, we should try to show love."

"Oh," said Little Cub. "Right."

"Grampa, could we ever do something
to make God *not* love us?"

"Nope. He always hopes for the best in us.
He sees a bit of himself in us. And that bit is love."

"How do we *know* God loves us?"
Little Cub whispered.
"I mean, when we can't see or
touch or feel him?"

"We trust he's always with us,"
Grampa whispered back.
"Like your brother and sister
can't see you right now,
but they know you're here.
That's faith. God tells us he
loves us, and he shows us his love
over and over again."

"How does he show us his love?"

"He reaches out to us in a hundred ways and through those around us…and it gives us that same warm and cozy feeling."

"Like family?"

"And friends, and our home, or even food on our table," Grampa said. "Every which way he can, God shows us his love."

"Most of all," Grampa said, "we know God loves us because he sent his Son to save us, to show us the way. And to help us when we don't make good choices. Because God loves us that much, we will never ever be separated from him."

"Whoa," Little Cub said. "That's a lot."

"Yes, it is. That's a God-size love."

Little Cub fell asleep thanking God for loving her.

She asked him to help her love others better.

She thanked God for her grandparents and parents and her friends and even the otters and her little brother and sister.

Because he had given her,
little her,
love.

Enjoy the rest of the God Gave Us series!

Available in eBook:

God Gave Us Christmas
by Lisa Tawn Bergren art by David Hohn

God Gave Us Heaven
by Lisa Tawn Bergren art by Laura J. Bryant

God Gave Us Love
by Lisa Tawn Bergren art by Laura J. Bryant

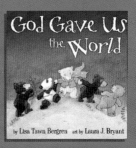
God Gave Us the World
by Lisa Tawn Bergren art by Laura J. Bryant

God Gave Us Easter
by Lisa Tawn Bergren art by Laura J. Bryant

Available in Print:

God Gave Us You
by Lisa Tawn Bergren art by Laura J. Bryant

God Gave Us Two
by Lisa Tawn Bergren art by Laura J. Bryant

God Gave Us Christmas
by Lisa Tawn Bergren art by David Hohn

God Gave Us Heaven
by Lisa Tawn Bergren art by Laura J. Bryant

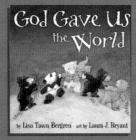
God Gave Us the World
by Lisa Tawn Bergren art by Laura J. Bryant

God Gave Us Easter
by Lisa Tawn Bergren art by Laura J. Bryant

A LIMITED-EDITION THREE-BOOK TREASURY
God Gave Us So Much
3-in-1 Treasury!

Available as Board Book:

God Gave Us You
by Lisa Tawn Bergren art by Laura J. Bryant

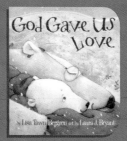
God Gave Us Love
by Lisa Tawn Bergren art by Laura J. Bryant